THE ZACK FILES™

A Ghost Named Wanda

For Judith, and for the real Zack,
with love—D.G.

THE ZACK FILES™

A Ghost Named Wanda

By Dan Greenburg

Illustrated by Jack E. Davis

GROSSET & DUNLAP • NEW YORK

I'd like to thank my editors,
Jane O'Connor and Judy Donnelly,
who make the process of writing and revising
so much fun, and without whom
these books would not exist.

I also want to thank
Jennifer Dussling and Laura Driscoll
for their terrific ideas.

Text copyright © 1996 by Dan Greenburg. Illustrations copyright © 1996 by Jack E. Davis. All rights reserved. Published by Grosset & Dunlap, Inc., a member of Penguin Putnam Books for Young Readers, New York. THE ZACK FILES is a trademark of The Putnam & Grosset Group. GROSSET & DUNLAP is a trademark of Grosset & Dunlap, Inc. Published simultaneously in Canada. Printed in the U.S.A.

Library of Congress Cataloging-in-Publication Data
Greenburg, Dan.
A ghost named Wanda / by Dan Greenburg ; illustrated by Jack E. Davis.
p.   cm. — (The Zack files)
Summary: Zack feels that a supernatural force is at work in his apartment when he encounters floating television sets, pancakes that flip by themselves, and a ghost named Wanda.
[1. Supernatural—Fiction. 2. Ghosts—Fiction.]   I. Davis, Jack E., ill. II. Title.
III. Series: Greenburg, Dan.   Zack files.
PZ7.G8278Gh 1996
[Fic]—dc20
96-7106
CIP
AC

ISBN 0-448-41261-6   **2004 Printing**

Chapter 1

When the first spooky thing happened, I didn't even realize it was spooky. I don't know why, because I happen to like spooky things...unless they're really scary I mean, in which case maybe not so much.

Oh, I better tell you who I am. My name is Zack. I'm ten years old. And I guess I've always been sort of interested in weird stuff. Stuff like werewolves and vampires and zombies and houses where you go into the bathroom and turn on the faucet and out comes blood. Stuff like that.

To be honest about it, I've never seen any of the things I just mentioned. But then I'm only ten years old.

Anyway, to get back to my story. One night a few months ago, I woke up suddenly. All the doors in our apartment kept on opening and closing. The door to Dad's room, my bedroom door, my bathroom door, the door to my closet. Just opening and closing by themselves. I figured, hey, no big deal. It's the wind or something. So I went back to sleep. If I had known what it really was, I probably wouldn't have been so casual.

When I woke up the next morning, the first thing I noticed was how messy my room was. Now I don't want you to get the

wrong idea. My room is always pretty messy. But this morning, it was a lot messier than usual.

The pants I had taken off the night before and thrown on the floor were now hanging from the roller of the window shade. The shoes I had tossed in the corner were in my wastebasket. My T-shirt was hanging from the light on the ceiling. My underpants were on my teddy bear's head. I was pretty sure I hadn't done any of these things. And I couldn't imagine who had.

I cleaned up the stuff as fast as I could. It wasn't so much because I like my room clean. I just didn't want my dad to come in and say, "What's wrong with this picture?" My dad is great, and I love him a whole lot. But he is kind of a neatness freak. And I really can't stand when he comes into my room and says, "What's wrong with this picture?"

As soon as I cleaned up my room, I went to brush my teeth. And that's where I noticed some more goofy stuff. Somebody had rubbed soap all over my bathroom mirror. And put Saran Wrap under the toilet seat. Had some kid sneaked in to play pranks on me? Or was something weird going on here?

"Zack, you up?" my dad called from the hallway.

"Yeah, Dad," I called back.

He stuck his head in my bedroom door.

"Uh-oh," he said.

I went back into my bedroom, and my mouth dropped open. My room was a mess again. Plus, all the electrical cords were tied into bows. And a framed photo of my Grandma Leah had a moustache and beard drawn on it. This was no kid playing pranks. Something weird was going on!

"What's wrong with this picture?" said my dad.

I could tell Dad was really upset by the mess. My mom and my dad split up a few years ago. Now I spend part of the time with him and part of the time with my mom. Dad's place has always been neater than Mom's. Up till now, that is.

"Dad," I said, "I just this minute cleaned my room, OK? Just before going into the bathroom to brush my teeth, I swear. I know this is going to sound crazy. But I think we're being haunted or something."

"Zack, I don't mind if you sometimes get careless and leave your room messy," said my dad. "But I really wish you wouldn't fib about it."

"I'm not fibbing," I said. "I really did clean up my room just a minute ago. I did not leave it like this."

The look on my dad's face told me he still wasn't buying it. But at that precise moment, the TV that sits on top of my bookcase floated gently into the air. Then it flew slowly and silently across the room and landed on my dresser.

My dad watched it go. His eyes were very wide. So were mine.

"You know, Zack," said my dad after a long time, "I think I believe you after all."

Chapter 2

Dad and I ran out of my room and escaped into the kitchen. We blocked the door with a stepladder. Then we turned around.

Yikes! It was even worse in here!

The table was already set for breakfast. The only thing was, it was set upside down.

The cupboards were open and empty. All the dishes were piled up in one very tall stack, which was swaying unsteadily back and forth.

There was no longer any doubt about it. We had a poltergeist. I've read books about this stuff, and I know. But in case you don't, a poltergeist is like a ghost. A ghost that likes to cause trouble. They usually appear in homes with families that have at least one kid, and they trash the place.

I looked at my dad to see how he was taking all of this.

"What would you think of our staying in the Ramada Inn tonight?" asked my dad.

"Oh, I don't want to spend the night in some strange motel room," I said.

Flapjacks began cooking on the stove. They flipped themselves up into the air. Then they turned over and landed back in the pan.

The very tall stack of dishes teetered in one direction, then in the other. Then it collapsed with a very loud crash. Pieces of smashed dishes flew in all directions.

The refrigerator door sprang open, and all the food inside spilled out onto the floor.

"On the other hand," I said, "I hear those Ramada Inns can be really nice."

Chapter 3

In school it was hard for me to do my work. And at the Horace Hyde-White School for Boys in New York City, there is a lot of work.

I kept thinking about ghosts. Who even knew what was going on now in my dad's apartment? I was thinking so hard about ghosts that I must have totally tuned out what we were doing in class.

At one point my English teacher, Mr. Hoffman, asked me something. I looked up, startled.

"So, Zack," said Mr. Hoffman. "What's your opinion?"

"My opinion?" I said. I cleared my throat and tried to loosen up my tie.

"Yes."

"Well," I said, stalling for time, "you know, sir, there are so many ways to look at that question. I wouldn't want to form an opinion too quickly."

"Zack," he said, "it's *my* opinion that you have not been listening to our discussion."

"Uh, no, I guess I haven't, sir," I said. "I'm really sorry. But I have a lot on my mind today."

"Well, thank you for being so honest,"

he said. "What's on your mind today that's more important than schoolwork?"

"Poltergeists."

Some of the guys started laughing.

"Poltergeists?"

"Yes, sir," I said. "Do you happen to know anything about them?"

"Well," said Mr. Hoffman. "I know the word means 'noisy spirit' in German. But what made you think about poltergeists?"

"Well," I said, "I know this may sound hard to believe. But some invisible force is wrecking my dad's apartment. And I thought it might be a ghost...a poltergeist."

The kids in class were laughing so hard they almost fell out of their chairs. "Oh, right, Zack," said some, and, "Yeah, sure, Zack."

"Anyone who believes in ghosts," said a

kid named Vernon Manteuffel, "is a super-stitious barfbag!"

There was more laughter.

"Shut up, Vernon," I said. Vernon Manteuffel sweats a lot and only takes baths on weekends. He keeps his bubble gum behind his ear. He brags that his gym clothes haven't been washed since the third grade. He's kind of a school legend.

"All right, boys, that's enough," said Mr. Hoffman.

"You probably believe in the Tooth Fairy, too," said Vernon Manteuffel.

"Shut up, Vernon," I said. I sure wish I could have thought of something cooler to say than shut up. But I couldn't.

"Why don't you *make* me shut up, barf-bag," said Vernon.

"Zack! Vernon!" shouted Mr. Hoffman.

"I do not tolerate fighting. One more word out of either of you and you are both staying after school."

Both Vernon and I got very quiet.

"That's better," said Mr. Hoffman. "You know, although I don't believe in the supernatural, there are a great many people who do. And they are not all superstitious barfbags either, Vernon. What I suggest, Zack, is that you go to the library and do a little research."

That was Mr. Hoffman's solution to every problem. Going to the library. Come to think of it, though, it wasn't a bad idea.

Chapter 4

After school I went straight to the public library. I looked up *ghosts* and *poltergeists* in the encyclopedia. It said some interesting stuff. But it didn't tell how to get rid of them. So I went to ask the librarian for help.

The librarian, Mr. Van Damm, has a thick moustache and very strong arms. That is because he likes to work out a lot with weights. He's a big, tough guy, but he really knows his reference books.

"Excuse me, sir," I said, "where exactly would I find stuff about getting rid of ghosts?"

Mr. Van Damm frowned at me. I hoped he didn't think I was putting him on. He didn't seem like the kind of guy who liked being put on.

"You're serious?" he asked.

"I couldn't be more serious, sir," I said. "We have ghosts the way some people have cockroaches."

"Then what you want is a banishing ritual," he said. "Banishing rituals are the Roach Motels of the spirit world. You'll find them under *black magic* over there under the stairway."

I thanked the librarian and went to look

under the stairway for books on black magic. In case you don't know, pulling bunnies out of top hats is called white magic. Putting curses on people or fooling around with evil spirits is called black magic.

I read all about poltergeists. In one book on black magic, I finally found a banishing ritual. You were supposed to light seven black candles and say this seven times:

"O evil spirit, O great and terrible demon that dwelleth in filth, that liveth in dark, stinking places, hear me now: I cast you out! I command you to depart! I order that you leaveth this place! O spirit who cometh in darkness, O demon of the foulest night, whose nose turneth backwards, whose face turneth upside down, whose clothes turneth inside out so that his underwear doth show, rouse yourself and be gone from this place immediately!"

It sounded to me like these evil spirits were all dead guys from ancient England or something. And maybe that was the only language they'd understand. I didn't think you'd need to talk to American dead guys like that. On the other hand, maybe the spirit that was trashing my dad's apartment *was* an old dead guy from ancient England. In that case, it would understand us.

I took my book to the checkout desk. I was in line behind a big kid who also had a load of books on ghosts and evil spirits. The kid was sweating like crazy.

"Vernon!" I said. "What are you doing with those books? You said anyone who believes in ghosts is a superstitious barf-bag."

Vernon's eyes bugged out when he saw it was me. He was so red in the face, I thought he might pop a vein. "I *d-don't* believe in that stuff," he stammered.

He sure didn't sound too convincing.

"Then why are you checking out books on ghosts?"

"If I tell you, do you promise to keep it a secret?"

"Maybe."

"Here's the thing," Vernon said, looking around nervously and lowering his voice to a whisper. "Something weird is going on in *my* apartment, too."

"You mean invisible forces have been trashing your place?" I asked, amazed.

"No, worse than that, Zack," he said. "Much worse. Invisible forces have been straightening it up."

"That doesn't sound so bad to me," I said, remembering what was going on in my dad's apartment.

"You don't understand," he said. "Things in my room are being invisibly rearranged. Not the way I want them, but the way something else wants them. I get out of bed; it makes itself. The sheets and blankets tuck themselves in so tight you could bounce a quarter on top of them. Sometimes that happens while I'm still in bed. Zack, do you think we've got a poltergeist?"

"If you do," I said, taking my book and heading toward the door, "it's even weirder than the one we've got."

"Hey, Zack!" he said. "Can't you help me?"

"I'll check in with you later," I said.

I left Vernon on the steps of the library. If the banishing ritual worked for me, maybe I'd show Vernon how to do it too. Not that he's my favorite person, as I said before. But I did sort of feel sorry for him —having to live with all that neatness, I mean.

I stopped off at the party store on the corner. I bought seven black candles. Then I headed over to my dad's apartment to do the banishing ritual. I wasn't all that hot to talk to dead guys, especially evil ones. But I felt it was our only hope.

Chapter

5

When I returned home with my book on black magic and my seven black candles, my dad was freaking out.

At first I thought he was mad at me for being late. But then I saw that wasn't it at all. Things in the apartment had gotten a lot worse. Not only was the place completely trashed, but there was clear gooey stuff all over everything. It looked like a combination of maple syrup and rubber cement.

"What *is* this stuff?" my dad croaked. He was so upset he could barely speak.

"I just read about this at the library," I said. "This is what they call *ectoplasm*. It's something that appears when there are spirits around."

I felt horrible for my dad and what had happened to his nice apartment. His eyes got kind of glassy. He looked like a guy in a war movie. Shell-shocked. Wobbly on his legs.

I knew I had to take charge. I showed him the book on black magic and told him we were going to do a banishing ritual. He nodded, staring straight ahead.

Then we lit the seven black candles. And I began to read aloud in a voice I hoped sounded more confident than I felt: "O evil spirit, O great and terrible demon that dwelleth in filth, that liveth in dark, stinking places, hear me now...."

I went on and on. But nothing happened. Nothing. So I stopped reading, slammed down the book, and looked at Dad.

"I'm sorry," I said. "This isn't working."

That's when we heard a very loud noise. A big bag of peanut M&Ms that was on a shelf just kind of exploded. All the M&Ms flew upward. They hit the ceiling, and stuck there. The way they stuck spelled out a message. It said:

OK OK, HERE I AM WHAT NOW?

"Oh, my gosh," I said softly.

"Oh, my gosh," said my dad.

I couldn't believe it. I had made contact with an actual evil spirit, with an actual spirit of a dead person.

If you want to know the truth, I got very scared. I felt a terrible chill, like I had just opened the freezer to get some frozen yogurt, and all of the coldness just fell out on top of me. The skin on my head and on my back and neck began to tingle.

"What do we do now?" I whispered.

"I don't know," said my dad. His voice was still kind of shaky. But he looked less dazed. "Why don't you ask it something?" he said.

"O spirit who dwelleth in this place," I said in a low, respectful tone. "Are you the same spirit who hath trashed our apartment?"

There were soft, scraping sounds as the M&Ms on the ceiling rearranged themselves into a new pattern. It said:

A RILLY DUM QUESCHUN

"I can't believe it," I whispered to my dad. "We're actually having a conversation with a dead guy!"

"Not only with a dead guy," said my dad. "With a dead guy who can't spell." At least Dad was sounding like his old self again.

"O spirit," I said, "why dost thou doeth these things to us?"

There were more soft, scratching sounds above our heads, and then a new arrangement of M&Ms:

FRANKLY IM BORD ALSO ITS FUN

"But you're ruining all our furniture and dishes and stuff," I said. "If thou keepeth this up, we'll have nothing left."

TUFF ITS MY JOB

"It's your job?" I said. "What's your job?"

More soft, scratching sounds.

2 B MISHEVUSS MISCHIVISS MISCHEFUSS O THE HECK WITH IT 2 MAKE A MESS OF THINGS

This evil spirit was about the worst speller I had ever met, alive or dead.

"Dad, I don't know what else to ask it," I whispered.

"We should find out whom we're talking to," said my dad.

"O spirit, what art thy name?" I asked. "I mean, to what name dost thou answereth?"

There was another quick arrangement of M&Ms:

WANDA

"Wanda?" I repeated. "But Wanda is a woman's name."

SO WHAT

"You're a woman?" I said.

SO WHAT

"Uh, about how many hundred years old art thou, ma'am?" I asked.

ABOUT 8

"Thou art eight hundred years old?" I asked respectfully.

NO JUST 8 SILY 8 AND A HAFF GOING ON 9

"Eight and a half?" I said. "Dad, it's a kid! A kid has been trashing our apartment!"

"Well, I guess that makes sense," said my dad. "I mean, it makes about as much sense as talking to dead people who speak through peanut M&Ms and who can't spell."

"If you're dead," I said, "why aren't you in heaven or someplace like that?"

LONG WATING LIST TO GET IN

"How come you chose this apartment to trash?" I asked.

I USE TO LIVE HEAR

"You lived in this building?" said my dad.

YEH ABOUT THIRDY YEARS AGO I HATED IT

"Why did you hate it?" I asked.

NOBODY TO PLAY WITH THEN ETHER NOBODY WAS MY FREND

I was trying to think of what to say to Wanda next, when suddenly my Game Boy went sailing through the air. It smashed into the wall and broke into around a thousand pieces. I loved my Game Boy. I had almost gotten to the 29th level of "Teen Masters of the Galaxy" on it. Now it was completely wrecked.

"Wanda, you jerk, why did you do that?" I shouted.

The M&Ms on the ceiling rearranged themselves again:

JUST FELT LIKE IT GOT BOARD

"You know what I think?" I said. "I think you're a troublemaker and a jerk. I think you were a troublemaker and a jerk even *before* you were dead. That's why you didn't have friends. You keep acting like a jerk and you're not ever going to have friends for the whole rest of your afterlife!"

Chapter 6

"Wanda seems to be an unhappy kid," said my dad. "Maybe I should try talking to her."

"Go ahead," I said. I sat down and crossed my arms. I wanted nothing more to do with Wanda.

"Wanda," said my dad, in this really calm voice, "I think you must be very angry to be trashing our apartment."

HA HA HA WHO EVEN CARES WHAT YOU THINK

"What do you think could be making you so angry?" my dad went on.

IM DED

"Well then, why don't you go and play with some nice *dead* girls and leave us alone!" I couldn't help yelling.

THERE AINT NONE AROUND

"Tough!" I said.

"Zack, you're not being helpful," Dad pointed out in a sharp voice. Then he turned his face back to the ceiling. "Wanda, what can we do?" he asked.

There was no reply for several moments. Then the M&Ms rearranged themselves once more:

I WANT ZACK TO PLAY WITH ME

I was amazed. I couldn't believe it.

"Why the heck would I ever want to play with somebody who destroys my toys and wrecks my dad's apartment?" I said. "You think I'm nuts? I only play with people who treat me nicely and who treat my stuff nicely. And that sure isn't you!"

Once again Wanda was slow in answering. Then the M&Ms shifted into a new combination of letters:

WHAT IF I COUD FIX IT

I looked at my dad. He looked around our wrecked apartment and shook his head sadly.

"Wanda," I said, "this place looks like a war zone. What you've done to our apartment is beyond fixing."

WANNA BET

"Yeah," I said.

HOW MUCH

"A quarter," I said. I took out a quarter and held it up. "Here's my money."

The quarter I was holding turned tingly and disintegrated. Then there was a blinding flash. All the pieces of my Game Boy flew back together again. It was just like in a TV commercial when they run the film in reverse and somebody jumps backward out of a swimming pool, onto the diving board.

"Holy cow," I said. "How did you do that?"

TRIX OF THE TRADE

"Listen, Wanda, could you fix the rest of the stuff you broke?" Dad asked in a hopeful voice.

THAT DEPENDS

"On what?"

ON WHAT ZACK DOES FOR ME

I looked at my dad. He shrugged. Then I had an idea. I didn't think I wanted to hang out with Wanda. She wasn't exactly my type, being dead and all, but...

"Hey, Wanda," I said, "if you fix the rest of the stuff you broke, I might just be able to find you a possible playmate."

YOU MEAN YOU

"No no, not me. Better than me. Somebody in the spirit world. What do you say?"

There was no reply. I wondered if Wanda had heard me. Then the room began to shudder, as if a major earthquake was about to begin. The whole apartment grew kind of hazy, like in a sandstorm. And then suddenly things started flying through the air. Dishes. Silverware. Plates. Pans. Clothes. Books. TV sets. There were horrid sounds. Scraping. Grinding. Clanging.

A heavy book bounced off my left shoulder. A glob of ectoplasm landed on my cheek. A small dish flew past my ear like a flying saucer. Come to think of it, it *was* a flying saucer.

And then, as suddenly as it had begun, it was over. The haze lifted. My dad and I looked around the apartment. We couldn't believe our eyes.

The gooey ectoplasm was completely gone. The kitchen was all cleaned up, too. In my room, things weren't what you would call neat. But it was certainly no messier than before Wanda had gone to work.

I was so happy I wanted to yell. My dad looked like he'd just won the lottery or something.

"Wanda, you did it!" I said. "You really did it!"

I TOLD YOU

"Well," I said, "you did what you said. So now I'll do what I said. Follow me."

WHERE WE GOIN

"You'll see," I said.

Chapter 7

My dad was so thrilled the apartment was back together again, he was happy to let me go to Vernon's. And when I called Vernon and told him I was coming to help him with his poltergeist, he couldn't believe it.

So I took my book of black magic and my seven black candles. And I walked the three blocks to Vernon's, looking both ways when I crossed the streets. I kept talking to Wanda. I wanted to make sure she was following me. I couldn't see her, of course. And because there were no M&Ms around, she couldn't "talk" to me. People I passed on the street saw me speaking to somebody who wasn't there. They looked at me like I was cuckoo.

"Yo, Wanda," I said, "if you're still with me, give me a sign."

A very stuffy-looking lady, wearing a straw hat with a wide brim, was walking toward me. All of a sudden something grabbed the brim of her straw hat and yanked it down over her eyes. Yep! Wanda was still with me!

A man smoking a fat, stinking cigar saw this and began to laugh. And then his cigar exploded in a shower of sparks, covering his face with black soot.

Soon I was at Vernon's apartment.

Vernon's folks were rich. Their huge Fifth Avenue apartment was filled with huge sofas, huge glass tables, and huge uncomfortable chairs. Most of their furniture was covered with clear plastic covers. Probably Vernon's folks sweated as much as he did.

Right away I saw the problem. His apartment was a lot neater than apartments ought to be. All the magazines on the coffee table kept rearranging themselves, first by size and then by date. And a dust rag with nobody holding it was polishing all the fancy stuff in the front hall.

"Hey, Vernon," I called, "where are you?"

The minute I said that, the dust rag stopped polishing and floated off down the hallway. It was going toward the back of the apartment. I realized I was supposed to follow.

Vernon was eating dinner in the kitchen, slurping up alphabet soup. As I watched, the letters in the soup kept rearranging themselves so that they went into his spoon in perfect alphabetical order.

"Zack, would you like some dinner?" asked his mom.

"No thanks, Mrs. Manteuffel. I think we should get straight to work."

We lit the seven black candles. Then I opened the book of black magic and began to read the banishing ritual again: "O evil spirit, O great and terrible demon that dwelleth in filth, that liveth in dark, stinking places..."

All at once there was a small explosion. A piece of paper dropped onto the kitchen table, and a pen flew out of a desk drawer and began writing in a very fancy handwriting.

"Kindly do not insult me," it wrote. "I am not evil. I do not dwell in filth. And I most certainly do not live in dark, stinking places!"

Vernon and his mom stared at the pen scribbling away on the piece of paper. Their eyes almost popped right out of their heads.

"Vernon," said his mom. "I didn't know you knew magic tricks. How did you do that?"

"It wasn't me!" said Vernon.

"Forgive me, spirit," I said. "I can see that you are very clean and neat. What is your name?"

"You may address me as Cecil," wrote the pen. "And by what name shall I address you, sir?"

"I'm Zack," I said. Nobody had ever

called me "sir" before. I sort of liked it.

"I am pleased to make your acquaintance, Zack," wrote the pen. "But whom have you brought with you? I sense the presence of another spirit."

There was another small explosion. A box of Cheerios fell out of a kitchen cupboard. Its contents flew onto the table where Vernon was eating his dinner. As Vernon, his mother, and I watched, the Cheerios arranged themselves into words:

HEY CECIL IM WANDA HOWYA DOIN

Chapter 8

The pen began scribbling messages to Wanda. And the Cheerios kept rearranging themselves into messages to Cecil. The scribbling and rearranging went faster and faster. Pretty soon it was too fast for any living person to follow.

"Well," I said, "I guess those two have hit it off."

The scribbling and rearranging of Cheerios skidded to a stop. Then the

Cheerios spelled out something slowly enough for me to read it:

THATS WHAT YOU THINK

"You mean you don't like each other?" I said.

The pen began to scribble again.

"Your friend Wanda is a crude, uneducated, and unacceptably messy person," it wrote.

The Cheerios came alive.

YOUR FREND CECIL IS A SNOB

"Hey, come on, guys," I said. "You two have so much in common, being dead and all."

"Yeah, you two *have* to get along!" Vernon added.

VERNIN YOU ARE A JURK WHO SWEATS A LOT, said the Cheerios.

"Hey!" said Vernon, getting up from his chair. "Take that back!"

Suddenly Vernon's pants were yanked down to his shoes. He had on underpants with purple dinosaurs. He quickly bent over to pull his pants back up. But before he could reach them, they were pulled violently up his legs and into place again. And his shirt was tucked in tight by unseen hands.

"Cut that out!" said Vernon.

"Stop that!" said Vernon's mother.

Vernon's pants were once more yanked down to his shoes. And then up again. And then down again just as fast.

"Wanda! Cecil! Stop it this instant!" I shouted.

It was louder than my dad yells when he's really angry. It was louder than Mr. Hoffman yelled when Vernon and I had our fight in class. It was so loud that Vernon and his mother were shocked into silence.

I guess Wanda and Cecil were too, because Vernon's pants stopped moving up and down his legs like a yo-yo. He pulled them back up again and sat down.

"That's better," I said. "You two may be dead, but you're acting like babies. And I will not tolerate it."

Mr. Hoffman likes to use the word "tolerate" a lot. I can see why.

"OK," I said. "Look, you two could be great friends. But you have to learn to get along. If you try to, you can. I mean Vernon and I are getting along now. And we don't even like each other."

"Hey!" said Vernon. He looked hurt.

"I mean we didn't *before*," I said. "Anyway, you have to get along. You don't have any choice. There just aren't that many dead kids in the neighborhood. Also, you need to find a place to stay."

HOW BOUT WE MOVE IN WITH YOU ZACK

"Yeah, Zack," said Vernon, "that's a great idea."

"Sorry, guys," I said. "No way."

"What about the two of us residing with Vernon?" scribbled the pen.

"Now *there's* an interesting idea," I said.

"No way!" yelled Vernon, jumping up from the table. For a moment there, I thought he was going to lose his pants again.

"OK, gang, I've got an idea," I said. "You know the Adventureland Amusement Park right across the river in New Jersey? Well, they've got a haunted house in it that is really pathetic. It couldn't even scare a five-year-old. But a couple of pros like you could really whip it into shape in no time. Why, after you two start haunting it, I'll bet that place could scare the daylights out of anybody."

OR THE PANTS

"Yeah," I said. "So what do you say, guys? Are you willing to move to Adventureland?"

There was no reply at first. And then: "I believe that taking over the haunted house at Adventureland would be an intriguing challenge," wrote the pen.

Vernon and his mom looked relieved.

"What about you, Wanda?" I said.

WOOD YOU COME TO VISIT US

"Uh, well, sure," I said. "You bet we would, Wanda. We'll visit you whenever we get a chance."

IF YOU DONT VISIT US THEN I GUES WELL HAVE TO VISIT YOU

"We'll visit you, we'll visit you," I said.

And so Wanda and Cecil went off to live

in the haunted house at Adventureland. I wonder if they found a way to get along! Every once in a while on the news, I hear about strange things going on out there. Everybody thinks the people who run Adventureland just dreamed up some new spooky tricks. But I know who's really behind it.

And I'm keeping my promise to Wanda. We're celebrating my next birthday with a big party in the haunted house at Adventureland.

It should be an interesting party. Very interesting, in fact.

What else happens to Zack?

Find out in

Great-Grandpa's in the Litter Box

I'd almost decided on that cute little tuxedo kitten when I heard the voice again:

"Hey, kid," said the voice. "I am *speaking* to you."

"Where are you?" I asked.

"Right here, dummy," said the voice. "In the cage in back of you."

I turned around. That scruffy old gray tomcat was staring quite crossly at me.

"You'll pardon me for hollering," said the cat. "But I was afraid you were about to make a terrible mistake and choose somebody else."